Nicholas Nickleby

Charles Dickens

Written by Julie Berry

Illustrated by Ismael Pinteño

Collins

Chapter 1

A boy and a girl stood outside a tall, dark house in London, and knocked on the door. On the corner, a gas street lamp gave a misty glow to the chilly winter afternoon. The boy, Nicholas, and his sister, Kate, set down the suitcases they'd been carrying ever since their coach from Devonshire had deposited them at The Dragon's Head Inn.

The boy's stomach groaned with hunger. Kate slipped her hand into Nicholas's. "Cheer up, Nicholas," she said. "Uncle Ralph is bound to offer us tea, and probably supper, too."

A man opened the door. Nicholas stared. Was *this* their Uncle Ralph? He seemed too old and shabby, with his spindly arms and legs and round potbelly.

The strange man gazed at them. "Yes?"

"Is this the home of Mr Ralph Nickleby?" asked Nicholas.

"It is," said the man.

"We're his niece and nephew," said Nicholas. "Our father has died."

The man's face fell. "Your father was a fine man," he said. "Come inside, and wait here."

3

Nicholas and Kate followed him into a gloomy hallway. After several minutes, the man shuffled back to them. "This way."

They followed him down the hall into a study. The room was dark, except for a low fire in the fireplace, and a green-shaded lamp on the desk where a man was sitting.

Nicholas and Kate approached the desk and took their first look at their father's brother. He sat hunched over his desk. He had their father's eyes, but where Father's had twinkled with kindness, Uncle Ralph's glittered coldly. The nose and mouth were similar, too, but there was no trace of Father's smile about this man's lips.

"Well," said Mr Ralph Nickleby. "So these are my brother's children."

"We are, if you please, Sir," said Kate.

"It does *not* please me," said Ralph. "Now I've seen you. What are you to me?"

Kate blinked. "Your flesh and blood, Sir."

He peered at her. "And?"

Kate's eyes were wet, and Nicholas himself struggled to blink back his own tears. Never had Nicholas imagined such a cold welcome from their uncle. They'd lost everything. Their home, sold to pay Father's debts. Their father, lying in his grave. And now their only hope was this man who sat there staring at them.

"Not full grown. Not much to look at," muttered Ralph. "What are your names?"

"I'm Nicholas, Sir."

His sister curtseyed. "And I'm Kate."

"Well," their uncle said, "and how do you plan to support yourselves now?"

Kate and Nicholas looked at one another in dismay.

Nicholas stood tall. "As he lay dying, Father made us promise to come and find you after he was gone. He said you'd look after us."

"Did he, now?" Mr Nickleby's brow darkened. "Why did my brother have children, I wonder, if he didn't bother to provide for them? He has the nerve to assume *I'll* pay their way? What gives him the right to decide how I spend my money?"

"It wasn't his fault he died, and left us poor," Kate said. "He provided for us well, until his business failed, and he died of a broken heart."

"A broken heart! Pah!" laughed Ralph. "No such thing. A broken head, perhaps, or a broken liver. But a broken heart? Hogwash. A poor excuse. He was too cowardly to face up to his troubles. But then, he always was weak."

Nicholas glared at his uncle. "How dare you speak of our father that way?" he cried. "We'll work to provide for ourselves."

Mr Nickleby laughed. "Oh, will you, now?" he said. "What can you do? Have you learnt any trades? Gone to school?"

"We've received all the schooling anyone our age could be expected to," Nicholas replied. "We're both good students."

Mr Nickleby rang a small bell on his desk. "In that case, I can get jobs for you. In my line of business, many people owe me favours. You'll both be hired. But see to it that you work hard and well. Don't embarrass me by being lazy or rude."

Nicholas was still too angry to talk, so Kate answered for them both. "We won't, Uncle."

The man who'd shown them in entered the room.

"Noggs, these are my brother's children," Mr Nickleby told him. "Naturally, I've no wish for them to live here. Take them to your lodgings tonight." He pulled two small coins from his pocket and gave them to his servant. "Use this to buy bread, if they must eat, and bring them back here at seven tomorrow morning. I can secure the boy a post as a teacher's assistant at Mr Squeers's school up in Yorkshire, and the girl can take a position and stay at Madame Mantalini's hat shop."

"You mean we won't be together?" Kate cried.

Mr Nickleby gave them a cruel smile. "Beggars can't be choosers, my dear," he said, "and you are surely beggars now. I'll get you jobs, unless you annoy me with selfish questions. Now, go with Mr Noggs, my servant, and do as he tells you."

9

Chapter 2

Nicholas and Kate arrived the next morning with Newman Noggs at The Dragon's Head Inn in Snow Hill. They found Mr Nickleby waiting for them.

He introduced Nicholas to a man breakfasting on eggs while three boys at his table shared one slice of bread and butter, and a mug of watery milk. The man wore an ill-fitting black suit. His greasy hair was combed over his head, and gruesome scars criss-crossed the place where one eye ought to be.

"Wackford Squeers," Ralph said, "meet my nephew, Nicholas, an orphan needing work."

Wackford Squeers rubbed his oily hands together.
"Enrol him in my school! For only 20 guineas per year,
he'll have a father in me, and a mother in Mrs Squeers,
at Dotheboys Hall in the delightful village of Dotheboys,
near Greta Bridge in Yorkshire, where youths are boarded,
clothed, taught, washed, furnished with pocket money,
provided with all necessaries ..."

"Nothing of the kind," said Ralph Nickleby. "I'll not pay
for him. He's been schooled enough to earn his own keep.
Didn't you advertise for an assistant at five pounds per year?"

Kate tugged on Nicholas's sleeve. "Only five pounds?" she whispered. "How can you live on five pounds?"

Nicholas shook his head. The sight of his new master filled him with dread.

Mr Squeers scowled. "I suppose he'll do."

Mr Nickleby turned to Nicholas. "See that you conduct yourself well, or I'll do nothing to help your sister." He left.

Anger boiled inside Nicholas. As bad as his new job appeared, he must make the best of it, for Kate's sake. He sadly bid his sister goodbye.

As they boarded the coach, a man hurried up with two small boys. "Mr Squeers!" he cried. "These boys! Can you enrol them in your school?"

"With pleasure," cried Mr Squeers. "They'll be boarded, clothed, taught, washed …"

"Yes, yes," said the man impatiently. "I'm Snawley. They're not my sons. I've never had a son. They're my wife's. We're newly married. She spoils them, Mr Squeers. Wastes all her money on them."

Mr Squeers's one eye winked. "I understand. For only 20 guineas a year per boy …"

"Only 20!" Mr Snawley beamed.

"A bargain if ever there was one," said Squeers.

"Send me the bill," cried Mr Snawley. "Don't be too easy on them. They need strict moral training. Even if you have to beat it into them. Ho! Ho!"

"Have no fear, Mr Snawley," said Squeers. "You've come to the right place."

Nicholas, however, felt with growing dread that he, himself, had not.

13

The ride to Yorkshire lasted two cold, snowy days.
Nicholas and the boys sat on top of the coach, with little
protection from the weather. If Nicholas thought the journey
was miserable, arriving at Dotheboys
Hall was far worse.

Everything Squeers had said about his school was a cruel lie.

Mrs Squeers greeted her husband, whom she called "Squeery", then raided the new students' luggage. Any clothes or toys that parents had sent for their children were given to their own spoilt son, Wackford. Any money parents sent went straight into Mrs Squeers's purse. Nicholas was horrified, but he was too tired to think. He went straight to sleep.

He woke in the morning to Mrs Squeers's voice.

"Where's the school spoon?" she cried. "If that Smike's gone and lost it, he'll sleep in the barn for a month."

"A school *spoon*?" asked Nicholas.

"It's brimstone morning," snapped Mrs Squeers.

Mr Squeers explained. "We feed the boys brimstone – that's sulphur – and treacle one day a month to purify their blood. Keeps 'em from getting ill."

"He might as well know the truth, Squeery." Mrs Squeers rummaged through every cupboard. "We don't care a fig for their blood. Sulphur and treacle cost much less than breakfast and dinner. Good for them, good for us. But I need my spoon to dose them, for those nasty, disobedient boys won't swallow it like they should."

Nicholas was horrified. "Who's Smike?"

"A wretched, stupid creature," said Squeers cheerfully. "He was a student, till his people stopped paying. Nobody claimed him. We keep him out of kindness, and make him work for us."

Nicholas rose, dressed, and followed Mr Squeers into the school room. What he saw made his heart sink.

The dark and dirty school room lacked most of its windowpanes. Paper patches were all that blocked the cold. What few school books Nicholas saw were old, torn, and stained.

But the room was nothing compared to the students themselves. They were the scrawniest, palest, sickliest children Nicholas had ever seen. They coughed. They stooped. They had vacant looks in their eyes.

Mrs Squeers entered the room with her brimstone and treacle. She pinched each boy's nose, tipped his head back, and shoved the spoon down their throats, heaped with her sticky, foul-smelling brew. Any boy who vomited the disgusting mixture back up was forced to swallow another large dose.

This was only the beginning of the horrors at Dotheboys Hall.

Mr Squeers had no business calling himself
a schoolmaster. He could barely read or write. He gathered
the pupils for pointless lessons lasting only a few minutes,
then sent the boys out into the cold to shovel snow, rake
stables and do other chores.

"That's what we call a practical education, Nickleby,"
boasted Squeers. "They learn more from experience than
from books."

Nicholas wondered why they wanted an assistant teacher
at Dotheboys Hall, if no learning ever happened there.

Each boy had only one thin suit of clothes to wear, day and night, and scarcely any blankets. They slept in a draughty dormitory, huddled against each other to keep warm.

Worst of all was the horrible way the Squeers family treated Smike. They worked him to the bone. Whenever chores weren't done to their liking, they denied him food, or banished him outdoors. Nicholas wondered how the poor boy stayed alive.

Nicholas went out of his way to smile at Smike, to say a friendly word, and if possible, to help him carry his burden of water pails or firewood. Smike began following Nicholas around and helping him in return. This made Mrs Squeers furious, and she punished Smike for it.

Nicholas endured the misery at Dotheboys for weeks. He didn't write to tell Kate about it. He didn't want her to worry.

Then one cold January day, Smike went missing. The Squeerses searched everywhere. Finally a student confessed to seeing Smike run away the day before.

Mrs Squeers sprang into her wagon and roamed the countryside in search of her runaway. After two days, she returned with a huddled, shivering form. She'd found Smike.

Mr Squeers bellowed for the boys to gather in the school room. Mrs Squeers dragged Smike in by his collar, while her husband thumped his ruler in his hand.

"Watch closely, boys," roared Squeers, "and I'll show you what happens to ungrateful, disobedient runaway brats!"

"Give it to him, Squeery," cried Mrs Squeers. "Teach him a lesson even he won't forget!"

Smike cringed at their feet.

Nicholas stepped forward. "Stop," he said. "You shan't punish poor Smike. I won't allow it."

He couldn't believe what he'd said. But there was no going back. And he wasn't sorry.

"What do you suppose," demanded Mr Squeers, "you can do to stop us?"

"He belongs to us!" shrilled Mrs Squeers. "We feed him, we own him! We can do with him exactly as we please!"

Nicholas stood straight and tall, and looked them both in the eye, despite his pounding heart. "No, you can't," he said. "It's not right. It's not decent. I'm sure it's not legal. And if you don't stop, I'll report you to the constables. They'll have a few things to say about how you treat these boys."

The crowd of schoolboys stared at Nicholas, and then at Mr and Mrs Squeers. This filled them both with fury.

"Into the basement with you both," yelled Mr Squeers. "We'll sort you out tomorrow morning, after a cold night sleeping with the rats."

"You can't lock me in," cried Nicholas. "I'm not a student. I work here, and I quit!"

"Oh, can't we, then?" sneered Mr Squeers. "Just watch me."

Before Nicholas could stop him, Mr Squeers had dragged him by the collar towards the cellar door, and locked him in with Smike.

Nicholas sat in despair. He'd lost his job. True, he'd hated it, but Uncle Ralph would be furious. Could he find other work?

Cold and damp seeped into Nicholas's bones. He searched for a way out. On a shelf, he found a box filled with tools. He fumbled in the dark, searching, until he found what he needed. A file! His key to freedom.

All that day, he filed away at the bolt on the loose, wooden door from the cellar to the yard. At last, after nightfall, when Nicholas's fingers were numb, the bolt gave way.

Nicholas whispered to Smike. "Come with me. We're leaving this place forever."

Smike grasped Nicholas's hand. "Come *with* you?"

"Of course," Nicholas said. "We'll stay together, no matter what."

Quietly, carefully, they tiptoed into the yard, out to the road, and off to freedom.

They hadn't gone far before they came upon a tall farmer leading his horse.

"Oho there!" he cried. "What's this? Be you runaways from the school?"

Nicholas froze. Would this man drag them back to Mr Squeers? There seemed no way to deny the truth. Nicholas nodded.

The man laughed and clapped his hands. "Runaways! That'll teach that rotten schoolmaster a lesson. Come with me, my lads, for supper and a warm bed. My name's John Browdie, and I'm so tickled at what you've done, that in the morning I'll send you on your way with a guinea in each of your pockets. Escaping from the schoolmaster! Ho, ho, ho!"

Chapter 3

Soon after Nicholas boarded the coach for Yorkshire, Newman Noggs brought Kate to Madame Mantalini's, a shop for ladies' fine hats and clothing. Ralph Nickleby met them and rang the bell.

A man wearing a silk dressing gown, Turkish trousers, and brightly coloured slippers answered. He boasted a splendidly thick set of black-dyed moustaches and whiskers.

"Oh, it's you, Nickleby," he said.

Mr Nickleby forced a smile. "May I speak with Madame Mantalini?"

The man beckoned them into the clothing shop. Elegant gowns of satin and lace hung upon mannequins wearing fancy bonnets with feathers, fruit and beads.

"My jewel," bellowed Mr Mantalini. "People here to see you."

Madame Mantalini appeared in a doorway. She was an elegantly dressed woman many years older than her husband, who had seated himself at a breakfast table.

"Why, Mr Nickleby, what a pleasure." She shook her guest's hand. "Who's this charming creature?"

"My niece, Kate," answered Ralph. "She's an orphan, and needs work."

"Oh." Madame Mantalini looked much less pleased. "You should've said so."

"I just did," said Mr Nickleby.

"Quite." Madame studied Kate, as one might inspect a goat for purchase. "Can you speak French?"

"I can," said Kate.

"Are you a hard worker?"

Kate bowed her head. "I've never had a job before."

"Which means," added Ralph quickly, "that she'll be ready to give it her all."

Madame Mantalini seemed unable to decide whether she liked Kate or not.

"Light of my life," interrupted Mr Mantalini, "there's a horse for sale at Scrubbs's, which it would be a sin and a crime to lose – going, my only joy, for nothing."

"For nothing," cried Madame. "I'm glad of that."

"For actually nothing," replied Mantalini. "A hundred guineas down will buy him: mane, crest, legs and tail, all of the utmost beauty. I'll ride him in the park. Other women will envy you, my idol. 'What a fine husband has Madame Mantalini', they'll say, 'and what a fine horse he rides!'"

"Oh, pooh." Madame Mantalini blushed. "We can't afford it, my dear."

"Just get Nickleby there to lend us some money, eh?"

Mr Nickleby coughed.

Madame Mantalini looked back at Kate. "Ah, yes. We employ 20 girls here, from nine in the morning until nine at night. Pay is between five and seven shillings per week, depending upon your skill. You'll sleep and eat here with the other girls."

Kate curtseyed. "Yes, ma'am. Thank you, ma'am."

"She can begin immediately," said Ralph.

Madame Mantalini ushered Kate into a workroom where 20 girls sat hunched over a long table piled deep with silks, velvets, wire, ribbon and trim.

"Girls, this is Kate Nickleby," said Madame. "Show her what to do."

Kate waited, hoping someone would greet her, or give her instructions. When no one did, she found an empty seat. Before her were piles of bonnets. By spying on the other girls, she saw they were trimming bonnets with brocade ribbon. She found a needle, thread and scissors and began to carefully follow their example. The whole lonely day passed until she could barely see to stitch. Kate climbed into her cot that night, wondering how to endure such unfriendliness.

The next morning, Madame Mantalini examined
Kate's work. "Not bad," she said. "You're a pretty girl. Here.
Put on this apron. You'll assist me with shop customers."

The other girls' faces blazed with jealousy. After only
a day, newcomer Kate had been promoted to the shop
floor, and called pretty, too.

For weeks, Kate worked in the shop with her mistress, fetching hats and scarves and bonnets. Each night she went straight to bed to avoid hearing the other girls' gossip.

Madame Mantalini modelled her fashions herself. One afternoon, an elderly lord entered with his new wife. Madame Mantalini demonstrated her most expensive hats.

"Not you, not you!" cried the crabby lord. "How can I tell if the hat will suit my bride when an ugly old thing like you wears it? Let that young, pretty girl try it on."

Madame Mantalini gasped. Her face turned pink. Kate wore the hats. Soon the lord and his wife left without buying anything.

"Think you're younger and prettier than I am, do you?" cried Madame Mantalini.

Kate took a step back. She'd done nothing to deserve this! Had Madame lost her wits? "No, ma'am," she cried. "I never said …"

"You think I'm an ugly old thing!" Madame stormed upstairs.

Soon two unpleasant men entered the store. They weren't shopping. They touched the hats and clothes as if they already owned them all.

"Girl," one of them said, "fetch Madame Mantalini."

"Tell your mistress," said the other, "that Misters Tix and Scaley wish to see her."

Kate passed along this message. Mr and Madame Mantalini hurried into the shop.

"Oh, gentlemen, please!" cried Madame Mantalini. "Give me more time to pay!"

"Your shop now belongs to us, ma'am," said Mr Scaley – or perhaps it was Tix. "You haven't paid your bills, and you've run up large debts."

Madame Mantalini scolded her husband. "Your spending has put me out of business!"

Mr Mantalini stroked his moustache. "Don't yell, my sweet. It's awfully unpleasant."

"Unpleasant!" shrieked Madame. "We're ruined! The shop is closed! The girls are all sacked, and must go home! Our names will be laughed at all over London!"

"Hush, my rosebud," said Mr Mantalini. "Only think, when we're not paying the girls' wages any more, I can buy that handsome mink coat …"

Kate slipped out of the door. There was no need to hear any more. As dismal as this job had been, now she had none, nor any home. Uncle Ralph would be angry, she was sure. Where could she go?

She looked up through the misty afternoon and saw an astonishing sight, the only one that could cheer her spirits then. It was her brother, Nicholas, hurrying down the street towards her.

Chapter 4

Kate and Nicholas embraced, and quickly told what had happened since they parted.

"No matter what," said Nicholas, "we must stay together from now on."

"Agreed," said Kate. "Forever." She noticed a thin boy watching them.

Nicholas smiled. "Kate," he said, "meet Smike, my faithful companion and friend."

"I'm so glad to meet you, Smike," she said. "Thank you for helping my brother."

They decided to go to see Newman Noggs.

Newman threw open the door of his apartment. "My dear children!" he cried. "What happened?"

They told Mr Noggs their tale.

He shook his head sadly. "If I were wealthy," he said.
"I'd gladly take care of you. I'm reduced to poverty by your
uncle. But let me offer you something to eat. The world's
a difficult place for young people with no parents to help
them." He wiped his eyes with his handkerchief. "Long
ago, your father was kind to me. I promise to do all I can
to help you."

"Thank you, Mr Noggs," said Kate.

"We mean to see Uncle Ralph tomorrow," said Nicholas.

"When he realises how bad the positions he found us were,"
said Kate, "surely he'll help us find something better."

Newman scratched his head. "I've known your uncle a long time. I wouldn't be so sure."

Next morning, Nicholas and Kate presented themselves at Mr Nickleby's office.

"What's this?" he barked. "Skipping work? Breaking your promise to me?"

"Uncle, please, let us explain," said Nicholas. "We worked hard, until …"

"Worked hard indeed!" snapped Mr Nickleby. "I've a letter here from Mr Squeers that makes it clear just how *hard* you worked. Attacking the schoolmaster! Striking him until he bled! Stealing money and jewellery from the Squeers family!"

Nicholas was too stunned to speak.

"That's a lie!" cried Kate. "Nicholas never did any such thing!"

"Kidnapping a student, one they held in their hearts like a son," added Ralph.

"Wackford Squeers," said Nicholas, "is the meanest, cruellest, most selfish, stupid ..."

"Insults won't excuse you," said Ralph with a sneer. "I should turn you over to the police. After all the trouble I took to help you, is this the thanks I get?"

"Trouble indeed!" said Kate. "You found us the worst jobs possible. If you cared at all, you'd never have sent us to such horrid places."

Nicholas held his shoulders high. "Never mind, Kate," he said. "He has no feelings. His head's full of greed. His heart's made of stone."

Mr Nickleby rose from his chair. "How *dare* you speak that way to me!"

"It's the truth," cried Kate. "We want no more help from you. You're no relative of ours. From now on, we'll look after ourselves." They left quickly.

Mr Nickleby sat down, seething with anger. *I'll get them*," he vowed. "They'll be sorry they dared speak that way to me."

Half an hour later, Newman Noggs appeared in Ralph's office.

"Don't bother me, Noggs," said Ralph.

Newman bowed. "Wackford Squeers to see you, Sir."

Squeers pushed past Noggs, sat opposite Ralph and grinned. *"I've got him."*

Chapter 5

Smike waited at Newman Noggs's small flat while Kate and Nicholas went to visit their uncle. He had a cough, but then, he'd had one ever since their journey from Yorkshire to London.

Smike knew Kate and Nicholas worried. He wished he could do something kind for them, after all the kindness they'd shown him. Smike was happier than he'd ever been. Nicholas and Kate wanted him to stay. For the first time in his life, he *belonged*. No one was mean. No one forced him to sleep in the cold. Nicholas shared whatever food he had with him.

Food! That was an idea. His friends would be hungry when they returned.

The little pile of remaining coins, from Kate's wages and Mr Browdie's guineas, sat on Newman Noggs's table. Smike decided to go and purchase his friends some lunch.

A London market was a thrilling place for a boy who'd never seen one, and never even held a penny. He felt rich as a king, with coins clinking in his pocket. He listened in wonder as the street vendors hawked their wares.

"Warm cider!"

"Hot pork pies!"

"Get your roasted chestnuts here!"

Smike's mouth watered at the delicious smells – cheeses and breads, meats and muffins, candies and soups.

The savoury smell of pork pie, with its crumbling crust, made up Smike's mind. He asked the pie-man for one, and dug into his pocket for the pennies.

"Gotcha!"

A loud voice burst upon Smike's ear. Rough hands yanked him around. His pennies fell to the ground.

"Oy there! Do you want your pie or not?" cried the pie-man.

But Smike couldn't answer. A sack had been thrust down over his head. Strong arms dragged him into a cab. Smike struggled, but he was no match for his captor. He huddled in the cab and waited in terror for the worst.

"Ain't this a stroke of luck," cried a familiar voice. "Won't Mrs Squeers be tickled pink when she hears who I found, all this way in London?"

Nicholas and Kate were surprised to find Smike gone when they returned home.

"The money's gone, too," said Kate.

Nicholas went to the window. "Maybe he went to the market."

They waited a long time for Smike to return. When he didn't, they ventured out to the market and asked vendors if they'd seen a boy like Smike. They had no success, until a pie-man said, "I saw a boy like that. He was about to buy one of my pies, when along came an ugly chap and snatched him away, neat as you please."

Nicholas could barely speak. "Please," said Kate, "can you describe the ugly man?"

"Greasy fellow," said the pie-man. "Squinty. Missing one eye."

"Squeers," whispered Nicholas. "He's in London."

47

They hurried home and waited for Newman Noggs. When they'd told him what happened, he looked grim.

"Squeers is in London, all right," he said. "He visited your uncle today. He always stays at The Dragon's Head Inn. Let's go."

They hurried across town to the inn and peeked through the window into the dining room. "I don't see Squeers," Newman said.

"Good news!" Nicholas whispered. "Farmer John Browdie is here!"

They entered and greeted Nicholas's old helper. He was astonished to see Nicholas.

"What brings you to London, Mr Browdie?" asked Kate, after Nicholas had introduced his sister and Mr Noggs.

"I came for a bit of a holiday," he said. "I wouldn't trade my farm for a London palace, but I do like a visit to town now and then, just to see the sights. I ran into Squeers here at the inn."

Nicholas and Kate explained what had happened to Smike, and why they suspected Squeers. Mr Browdie brought his great fist crashing down on to the table.

"He bragged earlier about capturing a runaway student. The monster!"

"Smike was no student," said Nicholas. "They treated him like a prisoner."

Mr Browdie leant over the table to whisper. "Listen here. He's got the poor lad locked in his room. It won't take me a minute to bust him out. But you've got to hurry away, the minute I set your friend free. Here's money for a cab. Keep your Smike where Squeers can't find him."

"We will," promised Kate.

Mr Browdie strolled upstairs to the guest rooms, and in no time returned with a terrified-looking Smike. Nicholas ran and threw his arms around him.

"Now, fly, you lot," said Mr Browdie, "and tell no one what I've done." He began to laugh. "I can't wait to see the look on the schoolmaster's face when he sees that empty room!"

Chapter 6

"I thought I'd lost you forever," Smike told his friends
that night.

"Squeers will never harm you again," Nicholas promised.

Smike may have been happy in heart and mind, but his
body was weary and ill from the fright he'd suffered.
His cough grew worse. When his friends offered him food,
he refused to eat. Kate urged him to go to bed early,
and he gladly did.

In the morning, Smike seemed no better.

"I'll look for a job today," Nicholas told his sister.
"Mr Noggs mentioned an employment agency."

Kate looked worried. "I'll look after Smike today,"
she said. "I'll come next time."

"That's good of you,
Kate," her brother said.
"I'm sure Smike will
recover soon."

Nicholas brushed off his clothes, combed his hair, polished his shoes, and headed to an employment agency. Inside he found a long line of people waiting for jobs, and a bored clerk sitting behind the counter, showing no interest in helping anyone.

When Nicholas finally reached the counter, the clerk greeted him. "What d'you want?"

"Please, Sir," Nicholas said. "Do you have any jobs for strong young men who can read, write, do arithmetic and speak French?"

"Of course we do."

That was encouraging. "May I look at the postings, please?"

"Oh," said the clerk. "We don't have any right *now*, if that's what you mean."

Disappointment welled inside Nicholas. He turned away.

"Positions are posted on the board outside," the clerk said. "Might as well look there."

The more he studied the job board, the more discouraged Nicholas felt. The positions all required skills and experience he didn't have.

Nicholas noticed another person studying the postings. He was short and stout, wearing a blue coat and grey trousers. What struck Nicholas most was the merry twinkle in the man's eyes.

The man noticed Nicholas watching him. Nicholas turned away.

"I'm sorry," he stammered. "I didn't mean to …"

"No harm done," said the man.

Nicholas liked his easy, friendly manner. "So many positions posted," he said.

"Aye, that there are," said his companion, "and so many more people in search of jobs. Poor fellows!"

Nicholas was puzzled. "Aren't you, Sir, in search of a job?"

The kindly man smiled. "Oh, you assumed I wanted a position?" He laughed. "I thought the same thing of you!"

Nicholas coloured. "Well, I do, in fact."

The man's eyes opened wide. "Surely not! A young gentleman like yourself should be in school! Shouldn't you?"

"I'm sure I would be, Sir," said Nicholas, "if my father were still alive." Immediately, he wished he hadn't told his private troubles to a stranger.

But the kind concern in the man's gaze soon eased Nicholas's mind. "What a shame, to lose one's father, and so young," he said gently. "Does your mother …"

"She's gone, too."

The man shook his head. "Any siblings?"

"A younger sister," Nicholas answered, "and a fellow orphan who's like a brother to us."

The man gestured to a nearby bench. "Please," he cried, "tell me all that's happened. My name is Charles Cheeryble. What's yours?"

Nicholas felt he could trust the man. Surely he couldn't make their sorrows any worse. He told him everything. Mr Cheeryble listened closely until Nicholas finished.

Then Mr Cheeryble leapt to his feet. "Come quickly," he said, "to my place of business. Here, we'll take an omnibus."

He hailed the bus and paid their fares, then got off at the Bank stop and led Nicholas to a warehouse on Threadneedle Street. The sign read, "Cheeryble Brothers". Mr Cheeryble led Nicholas inside.

"Tim Linkinwater, my good man," he called, "is my brother Ned available?"

"He's just finishing with Mr Trimmers," said the clerk behind a desk. "Trimmers is raising money for the widow and children of a man who died in an accident along the docks."

"An excellent man, is Trimmers!" cried Mr Cheeryble. "Put us down for donations also."

An office door opened, and two men emerged. It wasn't hard to guess which was Mr Trimmers, for the other was almost a perfect copy of Mr Charles Cheeryble. They had to be twins.

"Many thanks to you, Trimmers, for bringing worthy causes to our attention," cried Mr Charles. "And now, Ned, would you spare us a few moments?"

Mr Ned replied, "Charles, you never need to ask. Come in!"

The two brothers spoke privately while Nicholas waited with Mr Linkinwater. After not many minutes, both brothers returned, beaming.

"Master Nickleby," said Mr Ned, "my brother Charles has a very good feeling about you. I trust my brother's judgment completely."

"We feel," said Mr Charles eagerly, "that we should hire an intelligent young clerk to assist our dear Tim in his duties."

"My brother feels, and I agree, we couldn't do better than to hire you," said Mr Ned, with a smile.

"Therefore, we propose starting you," said Mr Charles, "at a salary of 120 pounds per year." Nicholas nearly fell off his chair.

"If you need a place to live," added Mr Ned, "we gladly offer our own home, which we share with two young people already: our nephew, Frank, and my brother's ward, Miss Madeline Bray. Both are about your age."

A great lump of relief and gladness swelled inside
Nicholas, fit to pop.

"And now," said Mr Charles, "we beg of you to consider
our offer. Take what time you need, of course, to think
about it, but we do indeed hope …"

"I accept!" cried Nicholas, leaping to his feet. "Bless your
kindness, good sirs. I accept!"

Chapter 7

Mr Charles and Mr Ned Cheeryble arranged that Nicholas, Kate and Smike should travel to their new home the next morning, by a cab sent to Mr Noggs's address. Bright and early, the three young people bid Newman goodbye, with promises to visit often.

When their cab arrived at the Cheerybles's home, a boy ran out bouncing a rubber ball, followed by a taller girl twirling a hoop. The boy threw open the cab and poked his face inside.

"Uncle Charles and Uncle Ned say you're to live here and be our new friends!"

His comical grin put them all at ease. The girl greeted Kate with a smile.

"I'm Madeline," she said. "I'm so glad you've come. It'll be lovely having a girl to talk to. Frank makes no end of noise."

Frank responded with cartwheels. Kate and Smike laughed, but Nicholas was too busy gazing at Madeline. With her long brown curls and her rosy cheeks, she was the prettiest girl he'd ever seen. He felt suddenly shy and awkward. Fortunately, Madeline was too busy talking with Kate to notice.

"Come inside," cried Frank. "Uncle Charles and Uncle Ned are waiting, and we'll all have breakfast together."

They found a hearty breakfast and a warm welcome. After eating, the Cheeryble brothers had a private talk with Nicholas.

"We've asked our doctor to visit Smike," said Mr Charles. He sighed. "You said his health was poorly, but I hadn't realised how frail he was until today."

"Thank you both," said Nicholas. "He was left to starve, almost, and made to suffer the cold far too long at Dotheboys Hall. Many of the boys there were ill and coughing."

"We wish to have that school investigated," said Mr Ned. "Who was the schoolmaster?"

"Mr Wackford Squeers," said Nicholas. "His school is in Dotheboys, Yorkshire, near Greta Bridge."

"Are you sure Smike knows nothing of who his parents are?" asked Mr Charles.

Nicholas shook his head. "All he remembers is that he was brought to the school by a man in a wagon, and that before that, he'd lived alone in an attic room."

"How dreadful!" replied Mr Charles. "We'll make inquiries."

The next several weeks were the happiest Nicholas and Kate had known since their father died. Their only worry was Smike's cough, which grew worse. But he was content. They all were. They fitted easily into the Cheeryble household. Frank's jokes made them laugh, and Madeline read to them from her marvellous collection of adventure stories. Nicholas worked by day, but there were stories and games after supper. Mr Linkinwater was so helpful as Nicholas learnt his duties that he found his working hours as pleasant as his leisure time.

Then, one day, Ralph Nickleby, Wackford Squeers and Mr Snawley – the man who'd got rid of his stepsons by sending them to Dotheboys Hall – appeared at the warehouse, demanding to speak with the owners.

Nicholas fought back his rising dread. No good could come of this.

"I see you've hired a criminal," said Ralph Nickleby to the Cheeryble brothers. "That boy, whom I'm ashamed to call my nephew, treated Mr Squeers shamefully."

"Stole from us," cried Squeers. "Money! Jewels! And this here man, Snawley's own son. We've come to fetch him back."

Ralph Nickleby pulled papers from his valise. "These papers prove," he said, "that the boy Nicholas kidnapped—"

"I never kidnapped anyone!" cried Nicholas. "You, Squeers, kidnapped Smike from a market, you foul villain!"

"See what a temper he has?" said Ralph. "The boy is dangerous. He snatched the lad from the school where he'd been sent by his loving father, Mr Snawley."

"That's right," said Snawley. "I … fell behind in my payments for a time, but as these documents prove, Smike is my own dear son."

"Why did you never visit him?" demanded Nicholas. "Never write? Never send so much as a coat to keep him warm?"

"We demand you release Mr Snawley's son to him immediately," said Ralph, "and release my nephew. We'll take him to the police to arrest him."

"Mr Cheeryble," said Nicholas to Mr Charles, "they're lying. Mr Snawley isn't Smike's father. I heard him tell Mr Squeers that he'd *never been a father*. He was *glad* to send his stepsons to Dotheboys where they could be educated so cheaply." Nicholas clenched his fists. "They educate the boys cheaply by neglecting them completely, and starving them to death!"

"Never!" cried Squeers. "At Dotheboys Hall, youth are boarded, clothed, taught, washed, furnished with pocket money, provided ..."

"Oh, stop it!" shouted Ralph. "Sirs, give us Nicholas and Smike, and we'll be on our way."

"We'll do nothing of the kind," cried Mr Charles. "Leave immediately, or we'll have you arrested for trespassing."

"We know all about you, Mr Nickleby," said Mr Ned. "We knew your reputation long before we met your excellent nephew. You shall have neither Nicholas nor Smike. Begone, Sir!"

The three men left, muttering threats. Nicholas sank into a chair. Would he never be rid of his uncle, and that horrid Mr Squeers?

"Have no fear, Nicholas," said Mr Charles. "We know he's lying. We've no intention of letting Mr Nickleby have Smike, or you."

"Thank you, Sirs," said Nicholas.

"Now would be an excellent time for Smike to take a trip to your beloved Devonshire," said Mr Charles. "Our doctor's worried about him. London air isn't good for his poor lungs. We'll rent a house, and see if fresh air can do Smike some good."

The next morning, the family took their journey into the countryside. They rented the very home where Nicholas and Kate had grown up. Smike loved exploring the places where his friends had spent their childhoods. But he couldn't walk about. Nicholas pushed him in a wheelchair, and soon, Smike kept to a bed. They carried a wicker couch into the gardens for Smike to rest on while he watched birds flit in tree branches, and rabbits nibble clover.

Nicholas showed Smike where his and Kate's father and mother were buried.

"Will you bury me there, too, when I die?" asked Smike.

Nicholas blinked back tears. He feared it'd be soon. The doctor said Smike's illness was called consumption, and it was destroying his lungs. He wasn't likely to recover.

Nicholas, Kate, Madeline and Frank all took turns keeping Smike company. One afternoon, as Nicholas sat talking with him, Smike let out a cry.

"What is it?" asked Nicholas.

"Over there!" said Smike. "In the trees! It's him, it's him!" He pointed. "The man who took me to Dotheboys Hall, years ago!"

Nicholas ran towards the spot, but he saw no one. He tried to reassure Smike, but the boy was too upset. Nicholas wondered if he had a fever, or was imagining things.

"Not to worry, my friend," he said kindly. "We won't let him harm you."

Then, one day, the worst came. Smike could no longer rise off his couch. He woke from a nap with a peaceful expression.

Nicholas said, "Smike, your sleep has done you good."

"I've had such happy dreams," answered Smike. "Such beautiful gardens, and such peace. I'm not afraid to go, now."

Nicholas realised what his good friend meant.

Smike took Nicholas's hand. "You've been the truest friend I could ever have."

Nicholas saw his friend's smile through his tears. "No more than you've been to me."

"I don't wish to leave you," said Smike, "but I confess, I'm happy to go."

"I'm glad." Nicholas wiped his eyes. "I'll miss you terribly."

Smike's pale eyes closed. "Give them all my love and thanks."

"I will."

Smike gave Nicholas's hand a final squeeze. "Remember me?"

Nicholas nodded. "Always."

So gently, quietly, like a baby falling asleep, Smike died.

Chapter 8

They buried Smike near Kate and Nicholas's parents.
Madeline wove wreaths of flowers for Smike's grave.

They returned to London, and slowly, life returned
to normal, though there was no normal without Smike
seated by the fireside.

Then one day, Ralph Nickleby entered the counting
office. Nicholas felt his skin prickle at the sight of
his uncle. Mr Ned Cheeryble beckoned them both
into his office. There they found Mr Charles and Tim
Linkinwater waiting.

"Mr Nickleby," said Mr Ned. "We've asked you here
on a serious matter. We know the treacherous things
you've done. But we believe in second chances. Do you,
Mr Nickleby, admit the error of your ways? Do you
apologise for the harm you've caused Nicholas, Kate
and Smike?"

Ralph Nickleby's lip curled in disgust. "I do nothing
of the kind," he cried. "I'll not be lectured by you!
I'm leaving at once."

"Stay," cried Mr Charles, "and hear the rest.
You must."

"We investigated your claim," said Mr Ned, "that Snawley was Smike's father, and found it utterly false. You forged those documents, and we have proof. We have statements from Wackford Squeers and Snawley, swearing they lied, at your urging."

"Nonsense!" said Mr Nickleby. "Squeers and Snawley would never …"

"Mr Squeers is in jail already," interrupted Mr Ned, "for crimes against students at his school, which is shut down. The students have been sent home."

"We've enough proof against you," Mr Charles said, "to send you to jail."

"I'm not afraid of you," snapped Mr Nickleby.

"Then perhaps you'll fear this," said Mr Ned. "We investigated your business dealings, and found that the huge investment you recently made, turned out to be a fraud. This very day, the news has broken. You just lost 10,000 pounds."

Mr Nickleby's face went pale. "Impossible," he stammered. "How could you know I made such an investment?" He wiped sweat off his forehead. "You're lying to frighten me."

"Indeed we're not," said Mr Charles. "I wish that were the worst news we must tell."

Mr Linkinwater left and returned with another man. Mr Nickleby looked as though he'd seen a ghost.

"My name's Brooker," said the man. "Perhaps you remember that, Mr Nickleby. You bribed me to hide your only son."

Mr Nickleby began to shake. "I have no son," he said.
"My only son is dead."

Brooker turned to the others. "Years ago, Mr Nickleby
married a woman, but forced her to keep the marriage
secret, lest her parents refuse to leave her any money.
Mr Nickleby wanted her riches, you see. They had a son,
but Mr Nickleby insisted the child be hidden, so their
marriage would stay secret. He hid the child in the attic in
his home. When the boy turned five, Nickleby forced me to
take him. I owed him money, so he could make me do his
bidding. He'd been so cruel to me when I struggled in my
payments, that I devised a plan to get even with him. I told
him his son had died."

He paused. "I'm ashamed of it, but it can't be helped.
I thought someday I'd produce his son and show him how
I'd got my revenge upon him."

"I sent his son to a cheap Yorkshire school, and paid
the tuition bill, until Mr Nickleby threw me in jail for my
late payments. The judge sent me to a debtor's prison
for years. I couldn't pay the school from prison.

When they released me, I returned to find out what had become of the child. At the school, I learnt he'd run away with another boy. I traced them to London, and from there to Devonshire. I finally got a glimpse of him, grown up, but sickly. I recognised him immediately, and he recognised me."

"I'd taken him to Dotheboys Hall, Mr Nickleby," said Brooker. "I named him Smike."

Mr Nickleby trembled in his chair.

"This boy, Mr Nickleby, whom you persecuted, was your own son," said Mr Charles. "You've lost everything. Your fortune, your reputation, and now, your only son. You'd already lost the friendship of your remarkable niece and nephew. Your boy could be beside you now, bright and healthy, if it weren't for your cold, greedy heart. A thousand times along the way, Mr Nickleby, you could've chosen kindness, and you'd be richer for it, in the love and companionship of family and friends."

"All this time, I had a son," Mr Nickleby whispered. "All this time." Then he realised the others heard him. "I'll hear no more of this!" he cried. "Say nothing more to me!" He jumped and ran out of the room.

When Newman Noggs arrived at Mr Nickleby's home the next morning, Mr Nickleby's office was empty. He went upstairs and found Ralph, still dressed, in a chair in his bedroom, stone dead. His face was fixed in an expression of grief and horror. Even heartless Ralph had died, it seemed, of a broken heart.

Mr Nickleby had indeed lost 10,000 pounds, but when his wealth was counted, there was plenty left. He'd left no will saying where his money should go, so it was divided between his only surviving relatives, Nicholas and Kate.

The Cheeryble brothers insisted Nicholas should leave his job, so both siblings could continue their educations. They assured Nicholas a position awaited him when he grew up.

Madeline and Kate became best friends, and Frank, a brother to Nicholas. Nicholas never stopped blushing at the sight of Madeline, but in time he could talk to her without tripping over his tongue. Someday, he hoped, he'd learn how to tell her how he felt.

Nicholas and Kate were grateful every day for the kind generosity of the Cheeryble brothers, who'd shown that family could mean more than blood relations. Smike, whose grave they visited often, had been family long before they learnt he was their cousin.

They erected a headstone over his grave that read, "Smike Nickleby, Cousin, Brother and Friend."

Uncle Ralph

Mr and Mrs Squeers

Snawley

Mr and Mrs Mantalini

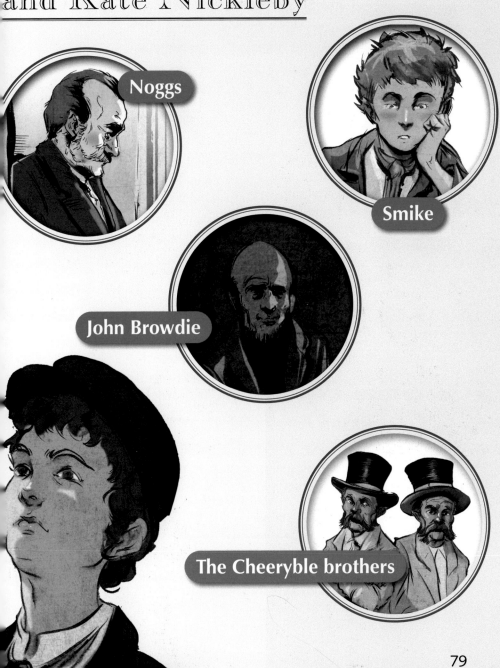

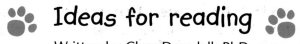 Ideas for reading

Written by Clare Dowdall, PhD
Lecturer and Primary Literacy Consultant

Reading objectives:
- identify and discuss themes in writing
- draw inferences such as inferring characters' feelings, thoughts and motives from their actions, and justifying inferences with evidence
- predict what might happen from details stated and implied
- identify how language, structure and presentation contribute to meaning

Spoken language objectives:
- give well-structured descriptions, explanations and narratives for different purposes

Curriculum links: History – social history (education)

Build a context for reading

- Explain that *Nicholas Nickleby* is a famous story by the Victorian author, Charles Dickens.
- Look at the front cover and ask children to describe what they think is happening in the illustration. Encourage them to make suggestions about who the characters are and what is happening to them.
- Read the blurb together. Ask children to think about how the characters' names are used to help us gain an impression of them. Refer back to the front cover and decide which characters are shown.

Understand and apply reading strategies

- Read the opening of the story to the end of p3. Ask children to briefly recount what has happened so far, and make inferences about the characters of Kate and Nicholas, and their situation.